I Grew With You

By SARAH MOLITOR Illustrated by ANASTASIA SIVURA

GOOD & TRUE
MEDIA

Images © Good & True Media
Edited by: B.B. Gallagher

ISBN: 978-1-7370796-2-0
Kindle ISBN: 978-1-955492-05-8
EPUB ISBN: 978-1-955492-06-5
Audiobook ISBN: 978-1-955492-13-3

Published in the United States by
Good & True Media
PO Box 269
Gastonia, NC 28053
www.GoodAndTrueMedia.com

Printed in the United States of America

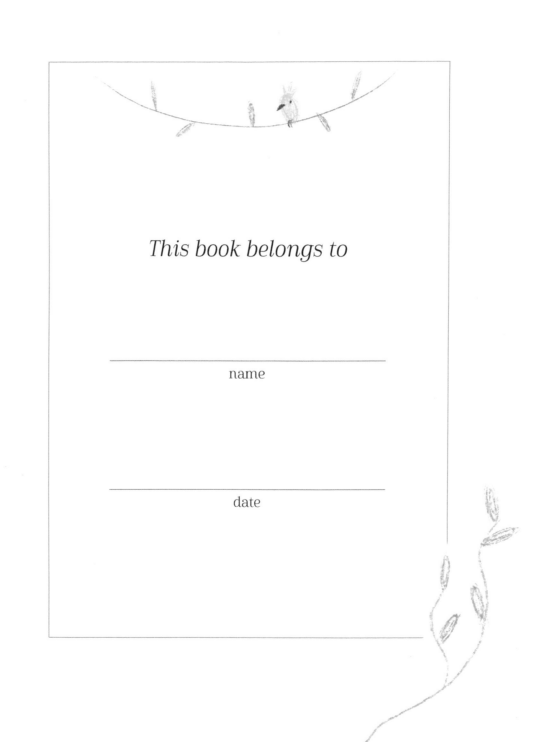

This book belongs to

_____

name

_____

date

Dear Mama,

I know one thing for sure: You are beautiful! And you are awesome! OK, that's two things—and there are actually a lot more. And how amazing is it that your little miracle grew with you and inside of you? Through each week, month, stage and all the crazy ups and downs you may have experienced, one thing remains: you were made to do this! You changed and stretched in more ways than one and I'm so proud of you!

As you read through this book my hope is that it reminds you of the beauty of the process and the bonding that happens between you and your little one. Some miracles take time and the miracle of motherhood is one of those! Each week and month of pregnancy comes with its own joys and growth. Through it all, not only is a baby formed but you as a mother are as well.

So whether you are at the beginning of your pregnancy journey, the middle, about to give birth, or have already experienced its beauty, I want you to be confident in this: you were given your child. You! Because you are exactly who they need. And that starts from the very moment your little one is formed.

I'm excited for you to cherish these pages and words as you read them to yourself or recount the experience with your children. May you smile, laugh a little, nod your head in agreement and cry with joy at all you have experienced. Treasure it forever as this is written from my heart to yours.

From one mama to another,
Sarah

P.S. Make sure you watch the birdies!

To my best friend and
husband Tim—you are the
best daddy to our boys!
And to Jude, Hudson, Chase,
Crew, Beck and our sweet
baby boy 6 coming soon who
inspired all these words—
I love you with all of my heart!

I could hardly catch my breath
cause two lines meant it's true.
A tiny one was growing
and that tiny one was you!

For a person so very small
you filled our hearts with joy.
We couldn't wait to meet you,
our little girl or boy.

And through each passing month,
I knew it to be true.
With the long road ahead,
I'd surely grow with you!

It was time to tell our news
to everyone we know.
We blew up big balloons
and put on quite a show.

Our family and our friends
all cheered for us with glee.
We couldn't stop smiling,
as happy as can be.

And through each passing month,
I knew it to be true.
The more we spread the word,
the more I grew with you!

Daddy left for the store.
It was six stores, in fact.
Since I asked him to buy
. . . ALL of the snacks.

Candy, chips and pickles,
three scoops of sweet ice cream.
Those days I was so hungry
that I licked my bowl all clean!

And through each passing month,
I knew it to be true.
The more my cravings changed,
the more I grew with you!

And then you started kicking,
a flutter soft and light.
But then you kicked and you kicked
and you kicked with all your might!

Those itty-bitty movements
throughout the day we shared,
were my favorite thing to feel
. . . a reminder you were there.

And through each passing month,
I knew it to be true.
The more you squirmed and turned,
the more I grew with you!

Finally, my checkup!
We got to take a peek
at all your precious features
like your little hands and feet.

They said you're growing strong
and you even waved hello.
You have your daddy's nose.
Just four more months to go!

And through each passing month,
I knew it to be true.
The more you formed in me,
the more I grew with you!

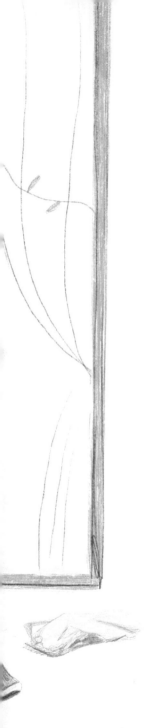

Guess what my little pumpkin?
You were growing oh-so-fast!
that my tummy popped right out
and my clothes just wouldn't last.

Sometimes the days flew by,
sometimes they went by slow.
But I loved every moment
that I watched my tummy grow!

And through each passing month,
I knew it to be true.
The more you stretched my jeans,
the more I grew with you!

We painted your nursery
and stacked up all your books.
We even built your crib . . .
it was harder than it looks!

We bought onesies and diapers
and a brand new rocking chair.
I couldn't wait to rock with you
and say our nighttime prayers.

And through each passing month,
I knew it to be true.
The more I said my prayers,
the more I grew with you!

I knew we were getting close.
I was up five times a night.
While daddy slept so soundly
snoring loud, tucked in tight!

I'd take a bathroom break
then watch a late-night show
or have a snack . . . or three
with just one month to go.

And through each passing month,
I knew it to be true.
The more you kept me up,
the more I grew with you!

And then something happened.
It quickly became clear.
With each breath I counted
the moment was now here.

I told your Dad, "it's time".
He loaded up the car.
On to the hospital,
it wasn't very far!

And through each passing month,
I knew it to be true.
The more I counted breaths,
the more I grew with you!

Then time stood still . . .

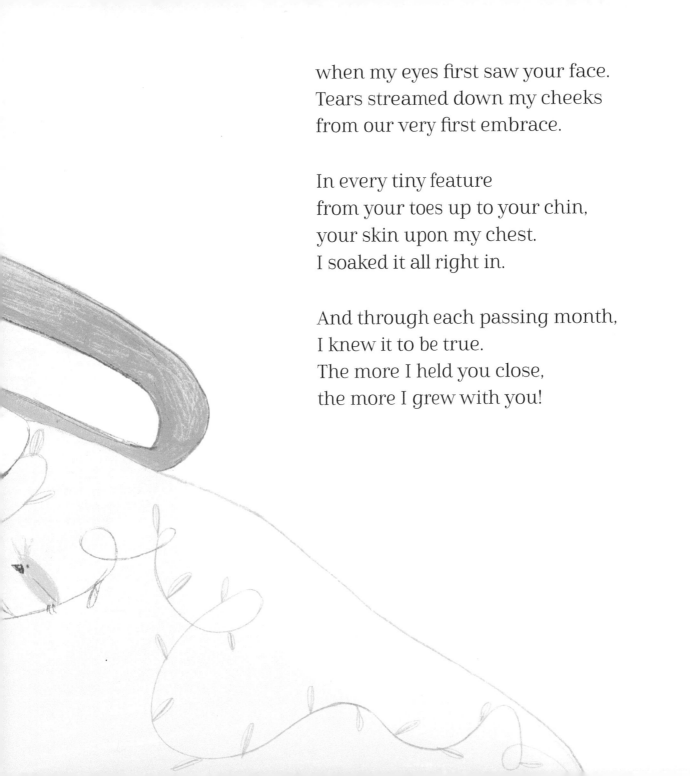

when my eyes first saw your face.
Tears streamed down my cheeks
from our very first embrace.

In every tiny feature
from your toes up to your chin,
your skin upon my chest.
I soaked it all right in.

And through each passing month,
I knew it to be true.
The more I held you close,
the more I grew with you!

At last we made it home
and now we're here to stay.
You snuggle up to me
and so we gently sway.

I'm rocking you to sleep
as I sing our bedtime song.
It's special just for us.
One day you'll sing along.

I have a lot to learn
but I know this to be true.
Our journey's just begun,
and I'll always grow with you!

SARAH MOLITOR is most notably known as "mommy" to her five (soon to be six) boys. Her role as wife and mother has shaped her more than any other title she has acquired. Along with raising her children, she also homeschools them full-time. She is the creative force behind @modernfarmhousefamily where she encourages, challenges and inspires her community on a daily basis. Sarah lives with her husband Tim and their growing family in Washington. *I Grew With You* is her first book.

GOOD & TRUE

MEDIA

Good & True Media aims to educate the imagination of children through fun, thought-provoking stories built on a strong moral foundation. We are dedicated to deepening the mind, moving the heart and strengthening the soul of children. We foster wonder in children so that they can pursue a virtuous life. By publishing new value-based stories with a strong moral message and by republishing classic works in a way that makes the stories of old new and accessible to a modern audience, we are able to be the positive influence parents need when entrusting their children to media.

Good & True is a proudly Christian company that seeks to shape the future of children's literature. Launched in 2021, we are only beginning our journey, but we pledge to remain steadfast in our core purpose—to help children grow in virtue.

For exclusive content, promotions, and sneak peeks of our forthcoming titles, subscribe to our newsletter.

SCAN ME

Lightning Source UK Ltd.
Milton Keynes UK
UKHW050403271021
392903UK00002B/47